CONFESSIONS

CONFESSIONS

VOLUME 2

A collection of erotic confessions

Selected and edited by Miranda Forbes

Published by Accent Press Ltd – 2009
ISBN 9781907016325

Printed and bound in the UK

Cover design by
Red Dot Design

Contents

LOUIS — Guernsey

The Knack

In my opinion, there's a knack to getting two girls into bed at the same time. It's got nothing to do with tricks or chat-up lines or anything like that. It hasn't even got that much to do with who you are, and if it's not good to look like Quasimodo, then it's not good to look like Adonis either. It's all down to how they see you.

Not that it's going to work every time. Most of the time, it won't, but some of the time it will and that's what matters. To get it right as often as it's going to go right, I reckon it boils down to just three rules and having the guts to say what you want.

Rule One: don't be the special guy. Most women want a man, and they want the best man they can get. Some men stand out, and girls talk – a lot – so in any group, there's usually one guy who's rated above all the others. If that's you, good on you, but I reckon I can do better. OK, so he gets lots of girlfriends, or more likely he gets picked up by the queen bee and has to spend half his time dealing with her jealousy. Maybe he plays around, but that's going to cause him a lot of stress. I don't want that. I want sex, and the dirtier the better. That's why I don't want to be the main man, the one all the girls are after. I want to be their friend.

Lots of guys complain that girls want to be friends but don't want to go out with them. That's fine by me. Who wants all that aggro? If you're her boyfriend, you have to take her out, and worry about other guys, and handle all that emotional stuff. But, if you're her friend, then there are all sort of interesting possibilities. Let me give you an example.

This was my first time, shortly after I'd qualified as a solicitor, and I had no idea it was going to happen. I certainly hadn't worked on it, and beforehand I'd always bought into the one guy/one girl myth. This was what made me realise there's a lot more to life. I used to go to a holiday resort on the south coast, a small place where everybody knew everybody else, pretty much. There were locals and there were summer visitors, most of who were regular. That meant there was a pecking order among the men, with the most attractive ones at the top. I wasn't exactly at the bottom, but I wasn't too far off it, and I used to be the one girls came to for male advice, because I was easygoing and friendly. I used to hate it before I knew how to take advantage.

Nikki was the daughter of a local hotelier, and she was gorgeous; medium height, very pretty, lots of thick, soft brown hair, a lovely, feminine figure, and tits like footballs. She was a contender for the cutest girl around. Sam was her best friend, small, pretty in a sort of freckly, mousy way, a nice bum and pert little titties, but not rated especially hot. Both of them were well out of my league.

Which was why I was walking both of them back to Nikki's Dad's hotel at the end of one slow evening, not one, but both. If I'd been the top dog, or even close, Nikki would have wanted me to herself, or let Sam go with me. With me, they both came, because nothing was going to happen, right? That's what they thought, and so did I.

We got to the hotel, around two o'clock in the morning. We'd already had a few drinks, and we'd been talking on the road. They wanted to grill me on what all the boys thought, and there was a lot to tell. So, we opened up the hotel bar and Nikki poured out Martinis. They went back to grilling me, and, after a bit, it started to get spicy. They wanted to know who'd done what with who, especially if there was any juicy stuff their friends had been up to but were too embarrassed to pass on. There was.

That's how we got talking about oral sex, not so much cock-sucking, but licking pussy. Neither of them had done it, and they were fascinated. I hadn't either, but that's one more thing, sometimes you need to be a liar, but no more so than the next guy trying to get into a girl's knickers. I told them I had, and that my imaginary girlfriend back home thought it was the most amazing thing in the world.

Both of them admitted they'd like to try it, and, well, we were all drunk, we'd been talking sex for hours, and I had nothing to lose. So, I offered to show them what it was like.

With almost any other guy, he'd either have ended up with one of them or been turned down because they didn't want to look cheap in front of each other and an attractive bloke. Not with me. I wasn't special, and that meant they went for it – both of them.

We did it in Nikki's bedroom. She was the leader, and the bolder, so she went first. I remember watching her squeeze out of those skin-tight jeans like it was yesterday, the shape of her hips, how soft her flesh looked, and, best of all, the way her pussy pouted out between her thighs. Sam was looking too, and I swear she was as mesmerised by her friend as I was, even if it was envy instead of lust, and who knows? Nobody said a word. I didn't dare, for fear of breaking the moment, and they were giggling plenty but didn't speak.

Nikki sat there, on the edge of her bed, jeans and knickers around her ankles, thighs apart to show off the sweetest little cunt. Down I went, and, if I'd never done it before, I'd read plenty. It worked anyway. She was in heaven from the moment my tongue touched her clit. There were no complaints when I slipped my hands under her bum, and when one of her hands went to her tits, I suggested she get them out, telling her I wouldn't mind, of all things! Out they came, so lovely, big and round and firm. She was holding them while I licked her, playing with her stiff nipples and giggling at Sam, at least until the pleasure got too much for her. Then she lay back on the bed, her thighs wide open, playing with her tits as I licked her out and felt her bum. I had to have those perfect titties in my hands, and took a risk, but by then she didn't care. She let me feel, and she put a hand on the back of my head to make sure I didn't stop until she'd come. When it happened, her whole body went tense and she was grinding her pussy in my face and panting like anything. When she'd finished, she was saying, "It's lovely, it's lovely," over and over again.

Sam was a bit shy about it, but she wasn't going to miss out – not after she'd seen what had happened to Nikki. She put her hands up her skirt and pulled her knickers off underneath, then let me put my head up it while she sat on the bed. I gave her the same treatment, licking as best I could and not pushing my luck until she was well turned on.

Like Nikki, I took her bum in my hands, but I've always had a thing about girl's bumholes, so when she was just about to come I put my little finger in hers. She called me dirty, but that didn't stop her coming.

I'd done them both and they were giggling and happy, Nikki still with her jeans and knickers around her ankles, although she'd put her tits away, Sam still knickerless. I told them what they'd done to me and took my cock out to prove it. They told me to put it away, but I begged them for a titty show to help me come. Sam called me dirty again, and a pervert, but they did it, sitting side by side on the bed with their tops pulled up to show off their titties while I tossed myself off on the floor. It only took a couple of touches.

Looking back, I wondered if maybe I could have pushed it further, maybe got a blowjob out of them, even fucked them both. It never occurred to me at the time. I just had to come, and I was very aware of how we stood socially. It never happened again either, or anything close, and they barely even referred to what had happened, except as "that night". They never told their friends, either, and of course, they didn't tell their boyfriends, which was just as well.

Rule Two: don't be a threat. Another thing about Nikki and Sam was that they both knew I wouldn't push them further than they were willing to go, and that's another important thing about getting two girls together. You mustn't be a threat, in any way. A lot of girls fancy hard men, dangerous men, men who make them feel scared as well as horny, and maybe guys like that sometimes can get two girls into bed, just by being such bastards. If that's your line, good for you, but for most guys, it's not going to happen. It's much better if you're seen as safe, maybe even a bit gay. Not too gay, mind you, because I knew one guy who played this trick and ended up having to go down on a gay friend's cock in order to watch two female friends get it on together. He did it, and he reckoned it was worth it, but I wouldn't.

I've played the harmless male friend card quite a few times, and got a lot out of it, but my best shot was with Daisy and Anna. I met them through a friend who was going out with Anna. They were very close and wanted me to come along and make up a double date. I obliged, even though it was a holiday romance and they were in Bournemouth, seventy miles away from my office at that time. We had a good time though and I even went out with Daisy for a few weeks, but it didn't work because we were just too far apart. My friend and Anna got quite serious, but eventually they broke up as well, and that was when I got lucky.

Anna wanted to know why she'd been dumped and got Daisy to ring me. I came down to Bournemouth for what I thought was going to be an emotional day with maybe a snog and a cuddle from Daisy at the end. By the time we'd left the third pub, Anna was past the crying stage and was cursing my friend with every word she knew. I was the good guy, the friend who'd come down to comfort her, and I was getting on well with Daisy too, even though she had a new boyfriend. That made me equal between them, and no threat.

Before long, I had my arms around both of them and that was fine. When I let my hand slip to Anna's bum there was no resistance, and when Daisy saw she complained that I was giving her friend all the attention. That's when I knew I was in, walking along the seafront with a nicely curved female bum in each hand. They were up for kisses too, and then snogging, first taking it in turns and then with our mouths pressed together, all three.

I never did work out if the two of them used to get dirty together. They never admitted it, but then I never asked. They were eager enough to snog, that's for sure, because when I tried for a suck of their tits, their mouths stayed together, and once I'd got their tops up, they stayed together, tit to tit at one side with my face between them as I took turns sucking their nipples. They were both quite big up top, but Anna more so, and I do love big, round breasts, ever since getting off over Nikki's, really. I had their nipples in my mouth and their bums in my hands, and it was getting seriously hot. They were both in jeans and I started to rub them, feeling the heat and wet through the denim, and if we hadn't been among some bushes on the Undercliff, I swear I'd have had them both then and there.

I got it further along, where the town finishes and there's no promenade, just dunes.

It was clumsy, messy and urgent, all three of us groping in the dark. They soon had my cock out, holding it together and trying to wank me off while I played with their tits. Their jeans came down too, both of them, bare bums and pussies all mine and nobody knowing whose fingers were where. I'm not even sure who was the first one to take me in her mouth, Anna, I think, but it might just as well have been Daisy. They both sucked me though, and I put it in both of them, with me flat on my back in the sand and the girls taking turns to ride on top. They'd got a condom on by then, and I could hardly feel a thing, but sometimes that's for the best. I just couldn't come. I wanted to, but I couldn't get the friction, which is why I got ridden so long, and why, in the end, Anna got on my cock and Daisy sat on my face. She knew I liked her bum in my face, and she'd told Anna, so they were both giggling like crazy, in between gasps and sighs.

Of course, I couldn't see, but I'm sure they were playing with each other's tits as they rode me, which made me even harder and more desperate, but Anna had started to wriggle around on my cock instead of bouncing up and down. She was trying to make herself come, and she got there, but it wasn't helping me, not without good, deep thrusts. That's why I got mine tossed off in her hand once she'd finished, with Daisy still on my face. The way things had gone made me feel like it was them having me, not me having them, but I didn't mind one bit, and when I felt myself start to come I stuck my tongue right in up Daisy's bottom. Both of them said I was a dirty bastard, and I am, which brings me to the next rule.

Rule Three: be a dirty bastard and make sure everyone knows it. There's nothing girls hate more than guys who look down on them for getting their rocks off. I can see why too. A guy has six different girls in a month and everybody reckons he's the man. Let a girl do the same and she's a slut, a slag, slapper and a dozen other nasty things, especially if she's done anything dirty. For boys, he can have as many as he likes, so long as it's all macho stuff, but let it get out that he's into anything weird or a bit gay and there goes his reputation as a stud.

I never had a reputation anyway, except for

being dirty, and while that's got me plenty of sneers and even a few threats, it's also got me a lot of very good sex. The thing is, girls are often dirty too, but they don't like to admit it, so if there's a guy around with a reputation as a bit of perve, but safe and friendly, and they want to explore their kink, then he's the one they go to.

Most of the time, it's just one girl and all very private and hush hush, a few quiet words to sound me out, a suggestion and back to her place or mine for a spot of what she fancies, maybe a bit of spanking or bondage, but I had one girl who wanted to piss on me. It can work with two as well, because if they know I'm a dirty bastard, they don't have to worry about their own behaviour. That was the way it was with Katie and Jane. They loved to show off, both of them, and to get men going but not actually put out. To do that, their favourite thing was to go to a car park where they knew there'd be men watching and get off together in the back. That meant they needed a driver, because neither of them drove and it would have been difficult anyway if they needed to make a quick getaway and they were in the back with their knickers around their ankles. That's where I came in. I had a car. I was friendly and wouldn't try to take anything too far. And I was a dirty bastard.

Of course, it also meant I got a ringside seat, and that would have been worth it on its own. They used to be dirty for the sake of it, not so much playing with each other to get off, as playing with each other to turn men on, because that was what gave them their big thrill. They'd pull up their tops and play with each other's titties, right by the window, or bend over the back seat with their bums on show, anything to tease the men, only you can imagine the view I was getting like that.

The first couple of times I kept my hands to myself, because that was the deal, front seat at the girly show in return for being driver and making them feel safe. Of course, they knew they got to me, just like they did to the men watching from the bushes, so the third time I said I was too horny to drive and I'd have to wank off before taking them home. They let me do it, both giggling like crazy as I tugged at myself and told them how gorgeous they were, and both of them still with their tops pulled up over their tits.

After that, it got to be regular. They'd put on their show and I could wank off if I wanted to as long as I didn't touch, or do it afterwards while they gave me a private viewing. It was Katie who first touched my cock, telling me what a dirty bastard I was and to hurry up as she leant forward from the back seat. She was topless, with one tit rubbing against my cheek as she took hold of me, pulling up and down like she was trying to get a boring but necessary job over with as quickly as possible. I came all over her hand, and I swear the disgust in her voice was for real as she mopped it up with Jane's knickers. The disgust in Jane's voice definitely was.

The next time, I asked Katie if she'd do it for me. She said no, but that it was Jane's turn. They had a little mock row over that, so I ended up sitting between them in the back, snuggled up close as they took it in turns to wank me and tell me what a dirty bastard I was for the way I was ogling their tits. From then on, it gradually got better, with all three rules in place, especially the one about being dirty. They knew I liked it like that, and they enjoyed seeing just what I'd do for my kicks. One time, they spanked me for being so dirty, and another time made me put on a pair of Katie's panties to drive back in.

When I admitted that I'd enjoyed being wiped down with Jane's panties she made me put them in my mouth while they wanked me off, waited until I'd come, mopped up and stuck them back in to punish me. Once they found they could make me eat my spunk, there was no stopping them, and it was after that it got really good. They'd put it on their tits and make me lick it off, giggling with disgust as they watched me lap it up bit by bit and swallow it. It was hard to get horny again right after I'd come, but the memory was always good for later, especially when they were now wanking me over their tits. The best, and one of the last, was when Katie bent Jane over the back seat and tossed me off over her friend's bum, then made me lick it all up out of her slit. I ate the lot and just kept licking, Jane's bumhole and pussy too, until she got there. Katie wasn't one to miss out and made me do her too, so at the end I had both of them bent over, their bums bare as I took turns to lick them from behind and played with my limp cock. For me, that was just heaven.

So there it is. You don't have to be Mr Macho, you don't need to learn any fancy lines or sneaky tricks, you just have to be friendly, safe and dirty and you'll get stuff other men can only dream about.

JIM — Basildon

Blitz Bums

I'm older than almost anybody now, so may have had experiences in which others would be interested, and which I would like to write down while I have the chance.

Things were very different before the last war, more different than perhaps you realise. I am always amused and a little irritated when I hear people making judgements based on modern morals but with respect to times past. Insulting the memory of Sir Winston Churchill, for instance, because his actions don't suit the modern moral perspective, which is just plain foolish. Make no mistake, he was a great man, and we'd be a sight worse off without him.

It was the same with sex. There was a great fuss made about homosexuality, for instance, which was illegal and pretty well unspeakable, although I dare say there were as many of them then as there are now, and not so very different in their tastes either. Other things you simply didn't mention, but no doubt they went on just the same, and it wasn't really considered done to boast the way everybody seems to nowadays. That doesn't mean it didn't happen.

I read somewhere that every generation thinks it invented sex, which always amuses me, and it's true. Looking back across my life, I can see it clearly. The 60s generation was the worst, so full of themselves, and so ready to look down on the very people who'd fought for them just twenty years before. They really thought they'd invented sex, and to hear some of them talk, it's a wonder the human race managed to get as far as it did. One thing's for sure, every one of them had a mother and a father, and they all came from the same place.

We weren't so very much better, I don't suppose. To us, everything from before the Great War looked old and staid, so that "Victorian" was said in the same way a young man or woman in the 60s might say the word "square", and the older generation made just as much fuss about jazz back between the wars as the next lot did about rock and roll in the 50s and 60s. All I can say is, there was plenty going on in my day, and if we'd didn't speak about it so much, that didn't mean it wasn't happening.

I suppose I was lucky, in a sense, although if I had a chance to live my time over, I'd want to be born thirty or forty years later than I was. The war caught my generation, and a lot of us died before we had a chance to grow up properly, but I wasn't one of them. I was in pest control, a rat catcher if you want to look at it that way, which was a reserved occupation, and gave me access to a lot of places other folk weren't allowed.

All that time, up until then, I'd never really thought of myself as a ladies' man. I was a bit shy, and spent a lot of time reading, which never did much to catch the eye of the girls. After the war broke out, it was all different. I was there, and so were they, and often enough with both of us scared out of our wits, which to my surprise made getting what I wanted a lot easier than you'd expect. Don't get me wrong, I never forced anyone in my life, but when a woman's trembling scared, it can be quite easy to slip a hand in where it might not otherwise be wanted, especially underground and in the dark. And where your hand goes one night, your cock is quite likely to go the next night, or even five minutes after.

There was another thing too. During the blitz, you didn't know if you'd be alive the next day, or the one after, or if you were, whether it wouldn't be under the Germans. That made it a lot easier for the girls to let their knickers down, and there aren't many men who won't take advantage of what's on offer, war or peace. Between my lot and the Yanks, I reckon half the people born during the war think their father is someone other than who he really is, if you get my meaning. I was always an optimist, me. I reckoned we'd come through OK, and I was more mindful than most of unwanted pregnancies, so I used to bugger them.

That may sound hard, but, like we used to say, one up the bum, no harm done, and it's surprising how many of them were all for it, at least, once they'd got used to the sensation. Girls who want to keep themselves pure for their husbands can have fun that way, too, but

I'll come back to that in a bit. First, I want to tell you how I used to do it. It's not always easy to get your prick in up a girl's bum. You may need to take her a bit by surprise, but once it's up I've generally found they like it. I always used to cuddle up to them, with her bum in my lap. That always got me hard, double quick, with a nice round bum nestled in my lap. You can kiss their necks easy that way too, which always drives them nuts, and, once they're randy, it's a great way to feel their tits and all. A little rummage, skirts up, knickers down, and when their legs come up a bit, you know they're ready.

What I used to do then is rub my helmet about in their slits, which makes them as randy as polecats and gets my cock good and slippery for where it's going. I keep on like that 'til they're moaning, maybe slip it in up their cunts once or twice, then bumps-a-daisy and I've got it in up their bum. Often they didn't realise I'd done it on purpose, which always gave me a bit of extra time to get it properly in, or if they did complain I'd start arguing the toss about not wanting to make them pregnant and that, which used to distract them while I got it stuck right up.

Like I say, once they've got over their surprise and sometimes a bit of shame, they're generally up for it, and come back for more as often as not. I'm quite small , which is an advantage as so long as I've got it nice and slippery in their cunts, it don't hurt. When I used to play for my local team I'd get laughed at in the showers sometimes, but I didn't care, because I'd just think of all those lovely round bums I'd had and all the lovely women who'd surrendered themselves to me.

You're probably thinking I'm a bit of a bastard by now, but that's just the way it was back them. The girls knew the score, and so did we, so if they didn't want a cock up them, it was best not to go off alone with a young man, and by the same token, if they went off alone with a young man, they expected a cock up them, although I admit not necessarily up their bums. Still, it's the way I like it, and I don't have to apologise to anybody, not now.

My favourites were always the posh ones. You might not think there'd be many, not down the East End where I used to operate, but you'd be wrong. Doing their duty they were, and I'll bet not one of the prissy little madams you see about the place nowadays would've had the guts to go within a million miles of the place. This was during the worst of the blitz, you see, when they were coming over just about every night, but we were getting used to it after a fashion, or at least we knew what to do. That said, it's amazing what human beings can get used to if they've no choice. It was the same in the trenches, so I'm told. The thing being with air raids, you get your head down sharpish, and you're not too fussy about where, or who with. Now on one occasion they came a bit earlier than usual, which rather took us by surprise, but by good luck I wasn't too far from a place where I had the key, an underground place.

I'll not say where, because with that and the date you could probably figure out who she was, and however big a bastard I may be I do keeps a lady's name safe. At the time all I knew was that I was about to shut the door when a girl comes running towards me with her coat held over her head, not that it would have done her a lot of good, but our guns had already started up and it might have stopped a smallish bit of shrapnel.

It was pitch black inside, with no way of making a light, and all I knew was I had a frightened dolly bird with me, clinging on like she was a drowning cat. I gave her all the comfort I could, as you do, and before too long we were kissing and I was starting to wonder if it might not be time to let myself in at her back door. I took it easy, because I could tell from her voice that she was posh, unusually posh, but she didn't seem to mind, and before long I had her knickers down and my hands full of the sweetest little bum I ever had the pleasure of.

She had a darling bum, that one, small and round and ever so cheeky, soft like a woman's bum should be, but not sloppy, and a shape that'd give a four-day corpse the horn. Now I reckon it's fair to say that by the time their knickers are down they're game, or why else would they let them down? So I turned her round and nuzzled it up between her cheeks, just to let her know what was coming, and when she stuck it out for more, that was that, she was getting it.

I gave her the usual treatment, pushing my

helmet in along her slit and wiggling it about, which got her moaning just like any other, and she was no virgin either, because when I pushed it in, up I went, nice and easy. She felt so good I could have done her that way, and sod the consequences, but I do like to do them up the bum and I couldn't let one like that get away without a buggering, not on your Nelly. So I slipped my cock out and gave her another rub, just until she was moaning again, then back he goes, all nice and slippery now, only not to her cunt, but right on her arsehole.

Took her completely by surprise I did. One push and I could feel her opening up around my meat, which is a feeling I love like nothing else. She gives a little squeak of shock, she does, and starts to move about, but that only encourages me. Oh, she was a right wriggler she was, squirming around in my lap and telling me I'd got it in the wrong hole over and over again, not cross exactly, more like in a panic, like when something's gone wrong and you have to point it out to someone ever so quick or it'll go a lot wronger. Of course I knew perfectly well I was in the wrong hole, because that's where I'd intended to put it all along, and with her little bum wiggling and jiggling about in my lap I wasn't stopping, not for anything. Women don't know what they do to men, they don't, wriggling their bums the way they do, and with my cock already half up I'd not have stopped if Adolf himself had come and tapped me on the shoulder.

I'd got myself about halfway up when she stopped fighting. Just gave in completely she did, with a long sigh. Then she calls me a name I'm surprised she even knew and sticks her bum out again, asking me to put it all in if you please. I tell you, just to hear her say that, in her soft, posh voice, that might have been enough to make me come, right then, if I'd wanted to. I didn't. I wasn't going to waste that moment. The bombs had even stopped, very courteous that was, I thought, and so I could give her my undivided attention.

Bent over a water tank she was, by then, with her bum pushed right out to let me in as deep as I could go and her tits in my hands as I buggered her. I don't think I've ever heard one moan so much, or use such language, even telling me how she could feel her ringpiece pulling about on my meat, and that's not something you usually heard from a young lady, not then, and I bet not now either. She felt so good too, all hot and tight up her jacksie, and her little soft cheeks pressed up against me, with my hands full of a pair of the sweetest little titties and all. I wanted it to go on for ever, but there's a point where you just can't hold yourself anymore, and I gave her my load, right up that darling little bum.

By that time the all clear had sounded, and as soon as we'd finished she smartens herself up, asks if I'll wait five minutes before leaving so we're not seen together, and thanks me for "comforting her", if you please. I never even knew her name.

Then there were my regulars. In normal times when a girl gets with you she wants you for herself, but those weren't normal times. Soldiers and sailors like to think the girls back home are being faithful and all, but it ain't necessarily so, believe you me. Only they don't want to get caught, or make a mistake, and that's where I came in. Three of them, there were, who once they'd got used to taking my cock up their bums just kept on coming back for more. There was Vi, my little blonde, whose old man was on the Rodney, her with sixteen inch guns and no arse. Vi had plenty of arse, like two piglets under a blanket. Just to watch her walk made me hard, with those cheeks wiggling about under her dress, and once I'd got her bare there was no stopping me.

I met her in a shelter, but we used to do our business at her place off Roman Road. She was funny, she was, very practical, but didn't like to talk about it, not straight out. Sometimes I'd meet her in the market, or down the Black Horse, but generally I'd walk up her road and if her nets were just a little bit open I'd know it was safe to come in and I'd be welcome. I'd knock on the door and she'd let me in quick for fear of nosy neighbours. We'd talk, just polite, over a cup of tea in her best china or a drop of something I'd managed to get hold of, and then get down to business upstairs, only not in the main bedroom, but a pokey little one she used to keep as spare.

Like I say, she didn't like to talk about it, so she'd always drop a hint, like saying she'd managed to get hold of some lard. That meant she had some between her cheeks and was ripe and ready for a buggering. Now I like to see what I'm doing, but she liked to do it in the dark, so we'd compromise, with the gas turned down low and I'd throw her dress up over her head so as she couldn't see. I can see it like it was yesterday, her kneeling on that bed, always ever so neat, her dress right up high and that lovely round bum sticking up under her slip. She'd stay just like that while I got her bare, bra off, slip turned up and knickers pulled down, so I could see it all and hold her knockers while I had her.

She always preferred to get herself ready, that one. Reckoned it was more ladylike, I suppose, so once I'd got her knickers down I could see the grease glistening on her ring, which was always just a little bit open, like she'd put her finger up, or maybe it was just because I had my cock up there so often. Anyway, I'd get myself hard over what she was showing and then put it up, nice and slow. She always used to try and keep quiet, like she didn't want to show how much she was enjoying herself, only she'd soon be moaning. She couldn't help it, and once I'd got right in, with a tit in each hand and my nuts pushed up against her fanny, then she'd let go, gasping and sobbing, but never once saying a word, except thank you, and that was once I'd done my business.

Janey was different, a right little tart. In fact she was a tart, sort of, because she liked a few shillings on the mantelpiece after we'd done it, whereas most of the others preferred presents. Not that it made any real odds on cost, and she'd have been worth double. That's the thing when you're paying for it, you can ask for what you want and you don't have to pussyfoot around. With Janey the light stayed on. She only had a couple of rooms, a bit off my usual stamping ground in a block back of Argyll Square with the bog on the balcony and the top of St Pancras Station sticking up over the block of houses opposite. She used to say it was like my cock and she ought to know.

She was proud of her body, Janey, and she liked to strip. I'd pick up a couple of bottles of beer on my way over and make myself comfortable in this tatty old armchair she had. She'd get my cock out and give it a quick wash with a soapy flannel, then a rinse, then a dry. I'd be half hard by then, what with the way she handled me, but sometimes she'd pop it in her mouth and give me a suck, just to make sure I got going. When I was nice and hard she'd open my beer for me and I'd settle down to watch her strip. She was good, very slow and she knew what I liked. Girls nowadays writhe around like they're trying to win a dance competition or something, and they're much too quick. Not Janey. She knew how to tease and she knew what men want. She didn't mind me touching neither, but then she knew the score.

First she'd take off her shoes, and believe me, the way she did that could've been enough if there'd been nothing else going. Woollen stockings, before the Yanks came over, nylons after, and she used to put one foot up in my lap and wiggle her toes on my cock and push down on my balls a little. Once she even got me right off that way, just to see if she could do it I reckon, with her dainty foot pressed onto my cock and balls and moving back and forth until I couldn't take it any more. Then she complained because I got it all over her stocking!

More usually she go the whole way, not

nude, because we didn't usually back then, if only because half the time it was bloody cold. She'd go down to her stockings and stays, with her fanny and tits showing and her bum bare behind. I reckon they look prettier that way. She always wore old-fashioned underwear, old-fashioned even then I mean, big knickers with a frill and a seam up the back, and a chemise instead of a bra. Watching her get her chemise off was always good, because she wore it under her stays to keep her comfortable and that meant tugging it out, which would make her tits jiggle like nothing else. Then there were the knickers, which she'd always leave to the last, then peel them down real slow with her bum stuck right out. Sometimes she'd tease, pretending to take them down a few times before she went bare, but she'd always go bare in the end.

By then I'd be raving, except when I couldn't hold it and had done it in my hand or all over the back of her knickers, which was quite often. She never took chances, Janey, and it was always straight up her bum. She wasn't like Vi, not at all. She'd spit on her finger, would Janey, and put it up her hole, right in front of me so I could watch, something else that used to make me pop my rocks quite often. Or she'd use her own juice, because she always got horny, but either way she'd be playing with her hole for a couple of minutes before she was ready.

Then she'd sit on my lap, the way a girl should, with a bare arse and a cock up her hole. I used to let her control it, because she liked to and because it felt dirty to have her easing my prick up her bum. She'd hold me with one hand, around my balls and cock so I was sticking straight up, and use the other to hold her cheeks apart, with two fingers so I could see her slippery hole and watch my cock go in, real close up, so I could watch her ring push in and then spread out to take me. One my head was in she'd feed me right up, slowly, only letting go when it was all in and she was sat down with her cheeks spread on my legs. Then she'd start to move, up and down, up and down, nice and slow, with her bum stuck out a bit so I could see. Sometimes I'd spunk, because it was just too much, but if I didn't she'd stop after a bit and sit bolt upright while she got dirty with herself.

That was always the best, if I could wait that long. A lot of girls had to be shown how to fiddle with themselves back then, and it was all a bit of a mystery. Not Janey, she knew exactly what to do, moaning and wiggling her bum on my cock while fiddling with her fanny, until she got there, and when she did her hole would go tight on my cock. That always made me come. It was like being milked up her bum, and I could never, ever hold myself back. She loved it too, and when she was done she'd give a little satisfied wriggle, and as often as not she'd leave it in while we had a cuddle and shared the rest of my beer.

She married a Yank in the end, and I was sorry to see her go, but the funny thing was, I remember him boasting about how she'd never been had, and he'd be the first. He was right, in a way, but if only he'd known he might not have been quite so smug.

COLIN — Norwich

The Erotic Ethics of Spanking Girls

It's not easy having a conscience, not for me. Unfortunately it's the way I am and there's nothing I can do about that. Nor would I want to, but I have a problem, which is that my personal ethics and my sexual needs don't match. That's because I like to spank girls.

It's not something I admit to many people, even now, because I know that most of them just won't understand. They think it's just some sort of perverted kick and that that means I'll do it when I can and whether the girl on the receiving end likes it or not, but it's not like that at all. Gay men used to have the same problem, that most people thought being gay didn't just mean you preferred partners of the same sex, but that it made you into some sort of homoerotic maniac, up for anything, with anybody and more than happy to stick your cock up any convenient arse without a second thought for the person you were buggering. Nowadays we all know that's crap, and it's the same with spanking. I would never, ever, spank any girl unless she was willing, and more than willing. Nor would I spank any girl if there was the slightest issue with her ability to give consent. But I do like to spank girls.

A lot of people also don't seem to get the difference between fantasy and reality. In fantasy it's fine to imagine a pretty secretary being put across her boss's knee to have her smart little office skirt rolled up, her knickers pulled down to the level of her stocking tops and her bottom smacked. It's fine to imagine her spanking being given in front of the entire typing pool. It's fine to imagine making her suck you off afterwards, on her knees with her red bottom stuck out behind and the tears rolling down her cheeks. It's even fine to imagine her getting it in the boardroom having her bent over the table for the entire senior management to take turns up her bottom hole. It's fine because it isn't real.

Reality is different, but it took me years to come to terms with that. I always knew what I wanted to do. It was a natural urge for me, something I had no control over, just like being gay, and like so many men who've had to struggle with being gay in a homophobic society, I was appalled. I wanted to be a civilised, caring man, dedicated to equality between men and women, which, by the way, I believe in absolutely. I also wanted to be accepted by my peers, as a free thinker, as a liberal, and as an egalitarian. That's not easy when you're having a conversation with a serious-minded young woman and all the while you're trying to fight down an urge to wonder what it would be like to tip her over your knee, flip up her miniskirt and pull down her little see-through nylon panties for a sound spanking in front of all your friends and hers.

This was in the sixties, and it was agony. It was a time of revolution, of student power, of a push to get rid of the old ways and bring in the new, and there I was, firmly in favour of change but all the time thinking that what the female contingent among my contemporaries really needed was to be lined up in a very, very long row for bare-bottom spankings all round. Then there were the miniskirts. The miniskirts were agony. They were supposed to be sexy, and they were deliberately daring, showing off a girl's legs and if she bent forward just a little bit her knickers too. To show that much was not only a fashion statement but a deliberate defiance of all that was prudish and old-fashioned, which included the idea that it's appropriate to punish a girl with a spanking.

And of course it isn't, but I wanted it to be, desperately, and it was impossible to reconcile that desire with my beliefs. So I kept my thoughts to myself, for years, allowing myself only the very occasional guilty relief over what were then quite rare pictures of girls being punished, most of which you bought in an envelope of a dozen from seedy-looking characters on the corners of Soho streets, although just occasionally one of the glossy men's magazines would devote part of an issue to the subject, and in time there were specialist productions.

That only made it worse, or at least it made my guilt worse, because just to know that pictures of some beautiful girl being put through the spanking routine existed was an exquisite agony. I had to have them, and yet I was convinced it was wrong. Again and again I bought packs of photos and magazines, only to dispose of them in a fit of guilt a few days later, and then to buy them anew, often the very same ones. The seedy men from Soho must have thought I was a lunatic.

Worse still, and this probably won't make any kind of sense to you, I used to have plenty of girlfriends. I'm a bit above average height, not bad-looking in a boyish sort of way, and I do try to be kind and considerate. In any case, I had no shortage of female attention, both at university and afterwards, and while I did my best to keep up what was considered a conventional relationship, with plenty of sex but only conventional sex, every instant was a keen agony, which was why none of my relationships lasted very long. It was easiest with the girls who were a bit shy or not especially conscious of their bottoms. I could handle that, in missionary position with the lights out, or even girl on top with the lights on, although it was never completely satisfying. The more liberated girls, who tended to be more aware of the appeal of their rear views, were far harder to handle. To have a girl on my lap and my hand on her lovely, soft, curvaceous bottom, mine to touch and stroke, that was agony. Looking back, I now know that some of them wouldn't have minded a spanking, especially if it was done gently, and some would even have liked the idea of being punished. At the time I not only assumed that no woman could ever desire such a degrading fate, but was absolutely determined not to give in to my perverted urges.

If just to touch a girl's bottom was a keen pain, then to take a girl from behind was agony. It wasn't actually that common in those days, when there weren't many sex guides around, or porn, and most people assumed that missionary was just the way you did things, but there are girls for who being in a crawling position for sex comes naturally, and who would offer themselves that way for sex.

It was so hard to resist, to be presented with that glorious rear view, a pretty girl on her hands and knees, naked or with her clothing dishevelled, her breasts hanging down, her soft, round thighs a little apart, her bottom lifted to offer her sex and also to let her cheeks come open and show off the tight dimple of her anus, to be able to enter her but unable to spank her first, and to try not to imagine what it would be liked as we fucked.

That was impossible. I had three girls like that over the course of the seventies: Linda, a slender blonde with a little round bottom that just cried out to be slapped; Laura, a bouncy little half Spanish beauty with huge dark eyes, voluptuous curves and a wiggle that used to make me stiffen at a hundred yards; and Paulina, a Jamaican girl with a mobile, meaty rump so full and firm it was as if she'd had her cheeks inflated with a bicycle pump. All three were very aware of their bottoms, all three preferred to get into a crawling position for sex, and I never spanked any of them. I could scream.

It was in the eighties that everything changed. I met Matthew. It was at a wine and cheese evening I'd offered to host for a local charity, and while I'm always very careful to keep my spanking literature under lock and key, I made one mistake. In a recent edition of my favourite there had been a particularly sadistic photo set, with a janitor not only spanking three college girls but making them watch each other being punished, parading them with their knickers down and their hands on their heads and finally making them wrestle, in the nude, after telling them that he was going to fuck the loser. As so often happened my conscience had got the better of me. I'd shredded the magazine and put it out with the rubbish, but as luck would have it Matthew volunteered to help clear up after my event, opened one of the tied bins bags in order to fit in some extra rubbish and saw the shreddings. He recognised the colour scheme of the cover, and when everybody else had gone he asked me if I collected the magazine, and, if so, did I happened to have issue 30.

I tried to deny it, but he knew, and he'd read the guilt in my face. Besides, this was the first time in my life I'd met anybody who shared my tastes and it was an immense relief to be able to talk about my problem. Matthew did not see it as a problem. In fact, he couldn't understand my point of view at all. To him, spanking was a normal part of foreplay, and something that he assured me the majority of girls enjoyed. I didn't believe him, at first, to which he responded by pointing out that he was married and had been spanking his wife, Margaret, regularly for the previous five years. I couldn't accept it, certain that he was abusing her, but our discussion had grown heated by then and when she came to collect him – and remember that we'd been drinking steadily all evening – he asked her straight out if she enjoyed her spankings.

She was deeply embarrassed, but when he explained the situation she actually got quite indignant and gave me a brief but pointed lecture on a woman's right to take control of her own body, as if I was some kind of chauvinistic dinosaur and her husband the conscientious liberal! In no time at all I was apologising and admitting that they were right.

Matthew worked near me and we were involved in the same charity, so it was inevitable that I saw him again. When I did I apologised once more and he assured me that it was of no consequence. This was lunchtime and we were in a quiet pub, so I jokingly asked him if he'd managed to track down issue 30 yet. He said he hadn't but was particularly keen to get it because his wife appeared in it. I dropped my pint.

He told me the whole story. She had always liked to be spanked, and like me had eagerly purchased the first specialist magazines when they came out, something I'd assumed no woman would ever do. Seeing an advertisement for models, she'd applied, and duly been photographed as she was put through the entire spanking routine, ostensibly for shop-lifting and by some dirty old man she'd never even met before. It had been in a dingy antique shop owned by the uncle of the magazine's proprietor, with her in a summer dress with polka-dot panties underneath, all in the classic sequence; accused of stealing, told off, given the choice between the police or a spanking, accepting her punishment, upended across his knees, her dress lifted, her panties pulled down and her bottom smacked, finishing with a shot that showed her red bottom and her pussy and anus stretched wide to the camera.

She had only done it once, not because she didn't enjoy the experience, but they'd quibbled about the money and taken ages to pay. I was amazed, not only that a woman could enjoy being spanked, which I still hadn't fully come to accept, but that she could take pleasure in the systematic degradation which to me was what pornography was all about. Yet from what she'd said when we met I knew that he was telling the truth and not merely trying to justify his abusive behaviour.

That meeting left me shaken. Their relationship challenged some of my most fundamental beliefs and it was also what I wanted, so badly. Before I'd always had the strength of my moral certainty with which to console myself that I was doing the right thing. That was gone, and in its place came doubts and a gradually rising regret for missed opportunities. I also had to get hold of issue 30, if it was the last thing I ever did.

It took me three months, of browsing in the cellars of the dodgier kind of vintage magazine shops, of scanning the for sale ads in my magazines, or standing at specialist market stalls in a state of near terminal embarrassment as the crowds ebbed and flowed around me. In the end I found the first forty-eight issues on offer at fifty pence each in an ordinary buy and sell magazine. I bought the lot.

The day they arrived was a Saturday, and

my first experience of spanking overload. The forty-eight magazines were in two large boxes and I unpacked them one by one, flicking through each as I did so. The effect was a parade of exposed and spanked bottoms, in every variety of female clothing and in every position: college girls in their uniforms with their skirts turned up and their panties pulled down, secretaries OTK to their bosses with their smart suits disarranged to show off bare pink bottoms, young nuns touching their toes as they waited for the cane with everything on show behind, ballerinas with tutus lifted high as they posed for punishment from stern mistresses, fetish girls strapped up tight for the application of a whip to their rubber-clad cheeks, wives rolled up by their legs as they were spanked in what I learnt was called the nappy changing position.

It got to me in a way that nothing ever had before, all that spanking, all those beautiful female bottoms, and then there was Margaret. She was a good-looking woman, but I'd only seen her in ordinary day clothes and no more than a touch of make-up. As a supposedly teenage punk shoplifter she looked impossibly exciting, full of attitude and cheek, pert and insolent, in short exactly the type of girl who would benefit most from a good spanking. And she had a lovely bottom, full and cheeky but in perfect proportion to her waist and thighs, and so firm that even bent across the elderly shopkeeper's knee her cheeks held their shape in a way to which no superlative can do justice. By the time I'd come three times I was in love with her and my head was so full of images of spanking that I felt dizzy and weak.

Those images would not go away. All night my dreams were full of girls being spanked, or prepared for spanking, or doing corner time with their smacked bottoms on show, anything and everything from that sadistic, perverted and utterly, breathtakingly thrilling ritual that is the classic English spanking routine. I couldn't keep my hand off my cock, and I masturbated until I was painfully sore and could no longer get an erection. I still wanted to come, but what I wanted to do more than anything else in the world was to spank a girl, and for true satisfaction it had to be Maggie.

That was not good. She's was Matthew's

wife for a start, and to approach her would have been a breach of ethics as unacceptable as what I wanted to do to her. Not that I could imagine her accepting in any case. Yet I had to have some sort of contact, if only vicariously, which was why I told Matthew that I'd got hold of issue 30. He was delighted, and immediately wanted to see it, but there was something else. I suppose I still hadn't got it into my head that women can really enjoy being spanked and even be open about it, but it had never occurred to me for a single second that Maggie would want to see the magazine too.

When Matthew came round she was with him. She even kissed me as they came in at the door and apologised for being angry with me the first time we'd met, saying she hadn't realised I was "one of us". I didn't know what to say, completely bemused by the idea of a woman not merely wanting to look through pornographic magazines, but with her husband and another man she hardly knew, and when she featured in one of the magazines, and not just nude, but with her bare bottom spread to show off her pussy and anus while a dirty old man spanked her!

It was the strangest experience of my life. They were completely casual, chatting happily about the weather and some road works they got stuck in on the way over, accepting drinks and sipping them, completely at leisure. I wasn't. I was shaking so badly I spilt the gin as I made Maggie her drink, and when Matthew coolly asked me to fetch the magazines it was all I could do to go through the motions, mechanically, barely able to take in what we were doing and quite unable to accept that Maggie really wanted to see the pictures.

They read the magazines together, first flicking through a couple of issues that happened to be on top, and then digging for number 30. I just sat there, hideously embarrassed, not knowing what to say or what to do. They didn't seem to notice, leaning close together and smiling happily as they leafed through the magazine until they found her photo set, at which she gave a gasp of delight, her hand going her mouth and her cheeks flushing pink, the very picture of embarrassed, excited femininity.

Matthew thanked me, with real feeling, but

Maggie was lost in the magazine, turning the pages with her eyes wide and her lips slightly parted, repeatedly giving little exclamations of shock and delight, ever more excited as she went through the sequence of her scolding, exposure and spanking. When she came to the one of her with her red bottom spread to the camera she was drumming her feet on the floor in sheer delight.

They went through the set a second time, and a third, drinking the pictures in, Maggie silent but for her excited little gasps, Matthew repeatedly saying what a bad girl she was for doing the shoot. He said she deserved what she'd got. He said she deserved more. He said she ought to thank me for finding the magazine by offering me the opportunity to punish her.

She stood up, she came over to where I was sitting, standing straight, her feet together, her hands fidgeting in her lap, her face downcast as if she were ashamed of herself. She called me sir, and she asked if I'd like to spank her bare bottom. I could only stare, at first at her, then at her husband. He gave me an encouraging nod and I did it. I patted my lap, signalling her to go over my knee.

It was my first time, after all those years of yearning and self-recrimination, and now I had a woman over my knee for punishment, a beautiful woman, and crucially, a willing woman. I took it slowly, savouring every instant: my first ever spank, delivered to the taut seat of her knee-length black skirt; her exposure, the pretty, respectable skirt rolled slowly up her thighs to show off first the tops of her hold-up stockings, then twin slices of creamy white, soft thigh, the tuck of her beautiful bottom and the underside of her lacy black panties, her full, feminine moon, a trifle plumper than when she'd been in the magazine eight years before but if anything more spankable still.

I spanked her on her panties, every smack sending a shock to my already aching erection. She was moaning and giggling, wriggling her bottom to encourage me, and yet deep within me there was still a voice telling me that she couldn't possibly be enjoying what was being done to her. It was Matthew who told me to take her panties down. Her response was a low purr, but still I hesitated, at which she stuck up her bottom and spoke two simple words, "yes, please". So I did it. I took hold of the waistband of those pretty black lace panties and peeled them slowly down over her peach of a bottom to reveal her completely, naked and glorious, her full, cheeky moon slightly parted to show off the tight brown dimple of her anus, and between her thighs the pouted lips of her distinctly wet pussy.

And I spanked her, bare bottom, over the knee, the classic pose, long and firm, with her husband watching in amusement and her moans and cries growing gradually more urgent, until at last Matthew declared that she'd had enough. I thought that was it, and my regret as she rose from my lap was a physical pain, but he wasn't done with her. He made her masturbate in front of us, with her skirt tucked up and her panties around her thighs, her bare red bottom showing to the room as she fiddled with herself until she came in a welter of shame and ecstasy.

He was grinning like a wolf as he asked, very casually, if he could borrow a bedroom for a few minutes. I could hardly refuse, and was left sitting there in an agony of frustration as I listened to her getting another spanking and then being fucked in the spare bedroom directly above my head. I'd have masturbated if I'd dared, but it was just as well I didn't, because Matthew came down alone and told me that Maggie was waiting for me and would suck me off. I could scarcely believe my ears, but I went, and she did, kneeling on the floor in front of the bed with her red bottom pushed well out as she sucked my cock, and all the while with her husband coolly sipping gin and tonic in the room below.

That was twenty years ago now and I have never looked back. In one drawer of my desk is a little note book recording all the names of the girls I've spanked, alongside a few details. There are twenty-seven different names, and my only regret? That I didn't start earlier.

ALISTAIR — Winchester

Strawberry Girl

I remember it like it was yesterday. She was called Poppy and she was the daughter of the place where I used to work helping look after the soft fruit. She was so fresh, and so lovely, blonde and beautiful, and such a bitch. She used to drive me wild. Unfortunately she was engaged, to the son of the owner of a local farm machinery hire firm, a good catch, or at least much better than me, a student with no particular prospects doing casual work on her father's farm to make ends meet until the following term.

That didn't stop me thinking about her, or watching her. She knew as well, and she used to dress to tease, and what with her father and I being the only two men working there I knew it was aimed at me. The shirts she wore were bad enough, or really the way she wore them, tied up under her tits with the buttons undone to leave her tummy bare and cleavage on show, so that you always thought that the next time she bent down to pick a strawberry her tits would fall out. Of course they never did, but if her shirts used to drive me to distraction her shorts were worse, because it wasn't so much a case of her accidentally showing off her bum as that most of it was on show already. They were cut-down jeans shorts, so tight they showed off every contour of her pussy at the front and her cheeks behind, or at least every contour that wasn't already spilling out at the sides, because they were not only indecently short but badly frayed. When she bent over she showed everything, and I do mean everything. She knew I watched, and if we were both working in the strawberry fields and her old man wasn't about she'd get into her tightest, shortest pair and then deliberately bend down in front of me, with most of her bum spilling out to either side and the frayed denim crotch pulled up so tight over her pussy so that the lips stuck out to either side, while if she straightened up suddenly and they went loose I'd get the full view, and she was always wet.

You'd have thought she was up for it, and I did, at first. When I suggested that she might like to nip up among the raspberry fences where we wouldn't be seen she told me in no uncertain terms that I could look but I'd better not touch, and that if I tried anything she tell her fiancé. He was a great red-faced thug, with a bitter temper and a reputation for getting into fights, which he won. I did as I was told.

After that she got worse, tying her skirts tighter still and wearing her shorts pulled up tight so that even just standing she'd make me shake with need, and she never lost an opportunity to bend over and show me what she'd got in even more detail. I hated it, but it was like a drug and I couldn't stop myself. Not that I had much choice with her working alongside me, and was technically my boss so I had to do as she said, something she never seemed to tire of pointing out. I'd have left only I needed the money and work was hard to come by, or at least I'd have tried to leave. I'm not sure I could have done it. I needed her, and she knew it.

She really did know it. She knew she had

me on a string and she also knew I was harmless, not just because I was wary of her horrible fiancé, but because I'm a gentle, passive person and it shows. I'm human though, and male, and believe me she drove me to the limit of my endurance over the course of that summer.

I couldn't help my reaction. I'd get hard, and she'd see, and laugh at me. I never did like to masturbate, because it makes me feel such a loser, and I hated the thought of masturbating over her. Only I couldn't stop myself. Just being with her made me ache with need, and by lunchtime I'd have blue balls, for which the only relief was a trip to the ramshackle loos and a couple of minutes of frantic tugging, all the while with her mocking laughter ringing in my head and pictures of her lovely body and the way she used to show off running through my mind. I'm sure she guessed, and whenever I came back from the loos she'd be wearing a little smile that was just pure contempt.

As the summer moved on she grew more confident in the hold she had over me, and bolder. One day when we were working cutting back excess foliage from the raspberry bushes she told me she was hot and was going to take off her shirt, and that I was to go into the next row and not to watch. If she caught me peeping she'd tell her boyfriend. I went, not one row away but several, because I knew I couldn't stand it. She ordered me back, telling me sharply to do as I was told. I had no choice but to comply, and to spend the rest of the morning working in the hot sun with her on the far side of the fence, topless, with her beautiful round breasts naked to the air, not fully visible, but not exactly invisible either, because I was constantly getting hints of naked, creamy flesh through the gaps in the bushes. She had me rock hard, and in the end I just couldn't stand it any more. I knew we were alone, we always were, so I moved a little way down the line, turned my back to the bushes and whipped out my cock, to jerk off in double-quick time to the images of her naked breasts that were flooding my mind. I thought I'd got away with it, because I'd waited until she'd gone to the end of the row with a bundle of cuttings, but even as I stood there with my eyes closed in pained ecstasy and the mess dribbling down my hand I heard her laughter from the far side of the bushes, as silvery and light as it was mocking.

After that I thought she was finally beginning to grow bored of tormenting me, simply because she'd pushed me to the limit and there was no more fun to be had. I could not have been more wrong. For a few days she was relatively well behaved, dressed as before but just ignoring me rather than deliberately teasing. I began to relax a little, until one day after work when she came up to me and told me that she was going down to the lake to swim, that she would be in the nude, and that if I tried to watch I'd be in trouble.

If she hadn't told me I would never have known. The lake wasn't somewhere I usually went, never mind after a hard days work when all I could usually think of was bed, and her body. She could have gone down there, swum naked for as long as she pleased and nobody would ever have been the wiser. As it was, I knew, and I had no way of fighting the ache that her words brought except to go down there.

I did not want to give her the satisfaction of knowing she'd got to me, and I definitely did not want her to carry out her threat of telling her fiancé, but I couldn't stop myself from going. To just walk there would have been foolish, so I set off down the road as if I was going down to the village, sure she'd be watching, and then struck off across the fields and around the behind the wood that bordered the far side of the lake. Once there I was more cautious still, going forward carefully until I'd found a place where I could look out from among the bushes with no risk of being seen.

She turned up a few minutes later, walking out onto the little wooden jetty at the far side, dressed in those same shorts and a red shirt on top. She was looking and listening, and I could guess it was for me. Something must have made her think I was watching, because she suddenly began to put on an act, first taking off her shoes and dangling her feet in the water, then untying her shirt and peeling it off. She spent some time like that, topless in the warm evening sun, deliberately posing to show her breasts off to best advantage, before suddenly lifting her bottom and pushing off her shorts. Nude, she stood up, disporting herself as if merely for the pleasure of being naked, but

71

knowing full well she was showing off. Again she spent a lot of time like that, before diving in, only to emerge from the water almost immediately, her lovely, naked body now dripping wet, and to dive in again. For a full hour she stayed there, deliberately showing off and no doubt imagining me among the bushes with a sore cock in one hand, because she knew full well that as long as she was naked I'd never be able to leave.

She was right, both that I couldn't leave and that I had a sore cock in my hand, because I'd come three times just watching her, and for all my rubbed skin and the ache in my balls I could hardly force myself to keep my hand away. She was wrong about where I was though, because the moment she was dressed she suddenly ran into a group of trees just to one side of the track that led back to the farm, only to emerge a moment later looking puzzled. She'd obviously thought I was hiding there and had hoped to catch me red-handed, and for all my frustration it felt good to have got the better of her at least in one small way.

Actually I'd done rather more than that. I'd hurt her pride. She really thought I hadn't been there, but she concluded, perhaps not surprisingly but I'm sure also because it was good for her ego, that the reason was that I was scared of her fiancé. I was, but I'd have risked ten of him to see her naked, and now I had, only she didn't know.

The very next day she told me that she was going to swim again that evening, and that she'd be naked. That wasn't all though. She asked if I'd like to see her naked, in that same mocking tone and quite obviously expecting the answer to be yes, or for my eyes, and my cock, to betray me if I tried to deny it. I did try, telling her she'd made me suffer enough and that I didn't care any more. It was the first time I'd actually admitted my feelings, although we both knew, and I swear that the cruelty in the smile she gave me on hearing my words wouldn't have been out of place on the face of a devil.

And yet I had planted a seed of doubt in her mind, because she made a point of telling me she'd be swimming that evening one more time, but instead of threatening me with her fiancé she simply told me that she'd better not catch me looking or she'd tell her father and get me sacked. That was altogether different, and it was a lie, because if there was one thing I was sure of it was that she loved to torture me, and if I got the sack it would all be over. That made me realise something else, that if she set her fiancé on me it would all be over anyway. He'd tell her father, and I'd be out, maybe not if it was just for looking at her, but definitely if it was for watching her bathe naked. I couldn't see either of them being too pleased about her going nude in the lake either, even if they would take her word against mine when she accused me of peeping at her.

I could have called her bluff. I could have said I'd be there and expected to enjoy the show. She'd have been furious, and maybe she'd have been powerless to do anything about it. But she wouldn't have gone down to the lake, and she might just have been spiteful enough to set her boyfriend on me to get her revenge. So I stuck with the same line and said I didn't want to see her anyway, which we both knew was a lie.

That evening I took the same route and hid in the same place, only this time she was already there, not on the jetty but in among the trees. I guessed she'd been watching the path, and obviously she hadn't seen me, which was presumably why she looked so indecisive, standing on the jetty and fidgeting, as if she wasn't quite sure what to do. After a while she ran into the trees again, came back out, took her shoes off and spent a while just dangling her bare feet in the water, then jumped up and stormed off. I was laughing.

The next day she was in her tiniest shorts and her tightest top, obviously determined to get a reaction out of me. She even flirted openly, which she'd never done before, asking if I liked the way she dressed and promising that the next time we worked up among the raspberries she go topless again as long as I promised not to try and touch. She also spent a lot of time bending over, as close to me as she could get, time and again showing off the bulge of her pussy lips to either side of the crotch of her shorts, down on all fours too, which was new and a view fit to make me burst. I took it all in, when I could, but pretended to ignore her and answered her teasing by telling her once more that I didn't care any more. Now she didn't seem quite so sure that I was lying.

The day after she arranged it so we were working among the raspberries. She went topless again, this time peeling off right in front of me and only then calling me a pervert and telling me to get into the next row and not to look. I just shrugged and went. That got to her, and at lunch she told me she was taking an hour off and would be sunbathing at the top of the field, in the nude. Again I shrugged, and even though it took all my willpower I took my own lunch in the orchard, well away from her.

The next day she had a new tactic. I was to rub oil into her back while she sunbathed in nothing but her shorts. I couldn't bring myself to refuse, for all that it meant she was turning the tables on me once again, but for all the pain of my frustration and my aching erection as I massaged her back there was a sense of triumph too. My hands were on her body, not that intimately perhaps, but touching her, and if her fiancé had known he would have been furious.

It was good for her too. She found a new game, and as always she wanted to take it further. Telling me she wanted to get a proper tan, she said she'd strip the next day, and I could do her back and legs, maybe her stomach, but if I let my hands stray elsewhere I'd be in trouble, while I was to wear a sack over my head to make sure I didn't peep. The sack was almost a humiliation too far, but the thought of touching her while she was naked was too much. I'd lost, once more her pathetic slave, and I would have to content myself with what she gave me, nothing more.

I did it though, letting her put the sack over my head and tie it off loosely to make sure I couldn't see. She made me kneel, holding the tub of cream while she undressed, and with every article she discarded she told me how she look, barefoot, and with no top, and naked, asking me if I'd like to see her breasts and bottom and pussy and then assuring me that I never, ever would and that I should have taken my chance to watch her swim.

Her voice was full of cruelty as she spoke, and of excitement too, while for all my humiliation my cock had gone hard in my pants. She saw, and laughed as always, calling me a pervert and little wanker, then once more warning me to keep my hands where she allowed as she got down. I had no choice but to obey and began to rub in the cream, first into her shoulders and neck, lower down her back, her calves and feet and thighs before she rolled over to let me do her front, all but her breasts and the triangular area around her pussy.

One touch and I'd have come in my pants, but I bit my lip, struggling to tell myself that it wasn't because of the way she tortured me that I was so turned on and determined to do my best to hide my feelings. She was just as determined to extract every last ounce of emotion, or so it seemed, demanding that I do her back and legs once more, only the second time as I kneaded her lovely supple flesh she had begun to sigh.

I took no notice, thinking it was a trick, only to have her suddenly say that I could do her bottom, her voice still rich with contempt, trying to make it sound as if she was giving me a privilege far beyond what I deserved, but there was something else there too. Just to touch those soft, smooth little cheeks was too much for me. This was sex, my hands on my darling's bottom and with that first touch my cock jerked in my pants and I'd come.

That didn't stop me. Now she was sighing openly and even though all my attention was on her bare and now well oiled bottom she seemed quite happy for me to carry on, at least until she rolled over and told me to rub cream into her breasts. Now there was no more dissembling. It was a straightforward order, not to torment me, but because she wanted her breasts touched.

I'd come, and that gave me control, allowing me to make it slow and sensual, gradually rubbing the oil in to those two lovely mounds, and when I deliberately began to play with her nipples her response was a low moan. I could have laughed. She'd sealed her own fate, demanding something too intimate to allow her to control her own feelings, while I'd already come in my pants and could handle my own. I took the bag off my head and there she was, my beautiful Poppy, naked and lovely, her head tilted a little bit to one side, her mouth open in pleasure, her legs ever so slightly raised and a little apart.

I went back to massaging her and now she was moaning openly, with her legs coming slowly wider as I rubbed her nipples and gently squeezed her breasts. With my heart in my mouth I began to go lower, still paying plenty of attention to her breasts, but allowing my hands to go every closer to the Holy Grail, her pussy. Her legs were apart before I touched that pretty pink slit, open and moist with her excitement, her bottom hole a tiny pink dimple between her sweetly turned cheeks. I put a little oil on her mound and there was no resistance, only a soft purr. I began to rub it in and still no resistance, but her legs came wider apart. I slid one finger into her eager hole and she moaned and arched her back.

She was ready for fucking and my cock had begun to grow once more. I wasted no time, determined not to spoil the magic moment as I stripped down my fly and pulled it all out. She saw, and for one moment there was something new in her eyes, not fear exactly, more a helpless resignation to her fate. She was going to get it too, because after all I'd been through there could be no more holding back.

I mounted her, and the ecstasy as I slid my cock in up that wet, willing pussy hole was beyond anything I'd ever experienced before, not just physical ecstasy but hot, singing triumph, and as I began to fuck her I could have shouted for joy. She was limp, at first, lying abandoned to her own needs, but as I picked up the pace in her cunt her arms came up and around me. We kissed, our mouths opening together and we were making love, properly, lost in our mutual passion as she lay spread-legged beneath me and I pumped my cock into her, harder and faster, lubricated as much by her own juices as the come on my shaft.

Only I'd just come, and I couldn't make it in that first flurry of passion. When I started to get dirty with her she just let it happen, too high to even think of her dignity. I fucked her on her knees and I rubbed my cock in the slit of her bum. I made her suck me and I fucked her between her tits. I had her mount up on top of me and told her to play with her cunt while she pleasured my cock. She did it. She did it all. She made herself come and she cried out my name in her ecstasy, and when she was done she knelt on all fours at my command and let me spunk over her bottom. That was perfect, to have her kneeling to my orders, her beautiful little bottom turned up under my cock, her pussy agape and soaking, her bumhole twitching as I spattered her lovely cheeks with hot white droplets, that really was perfect, the perfect ecstasy and the perfect revenge.

That was near the end of summer and it never happened again, but I'd broken her spell and after that we were friends, if a little wary of each other. Just over a week later I went back to university, and that would have been that, but for a chance wrong turning that took me past the farm the other day. I stopped, telling myself I'd buy some strawberries, and maybe get a glimpse of my strawberry girl, or find out what had happened.

And there she was, ten years older but still beautiful, her perky breasts now full and heavy but still held up in a tight red shirt, her hips wide and her bottom just nicely chubby, and still packed into tiny blue denim shorts. Her husband was with her too, his massive bulk still alarming, but not his ready smile for a wealthy customer, nor the fringe of sandy-coloured scruff which was all that remained of his hair. They'd had children too, six of them, three little girls and three little boys, all blonde and healthy like their parents, except the eldest, a dark-haired boy with a thin body and intelligent eyes not entirely unlike my own.

Looking for love? Our unique dating sites offer the perfect way to meet someone who shares your fantasies.

www.xcitedating.com

Find someone who'll turn fiction into reality and make your fantasies come true.

www.xcitespanking.com

Spanking is our most popular theme – here's the place to find out why!

www.girlfun-dating.co.uk

Lesbian dating for girls who wanna have fun!

www.ultimatecurves.com

For sexy, curvy girls and the men who love them.

Also available at £2.99

Confessions Volume 1

Some experiences just have to be confessed!

When a voyeur discovers a secret oasis of naked sunbathing girls, it's not long before the watched turn the tables on the watcher...

After learning the art of rope-play and a woman's love of vibrations in a special place, there's a guy who can get a girl to do anything, even in public ...

Who would have guessed that an uptight female teacher had such outrageous tastes? But the guy who thawed the ice-maiden learns that dirt has a special appeal ...

Hell hath no fury like a woman scorned; the trick is to learn how to love it ...

ISBN 9781907016318